PLEASE
WASH YOUR HANDS
BEFORE HANDLING

the Trouble with Wishes

Diane Stanley

◾ HarperCollinsPublishers

Jane wished she could be just like Pyg.

Not in every way, of course. She didn't want to be a boy, for instance, or have ears that stuck out, or be allergic to cats.

No, what Jane really wanted, more than anything in the world, was to be able to do what Pyg could do—take a hunk of stone, a hammer, and a chisel and carve a lion that looked so real you could practically feel its hot breath and hear its terrible roar.

Jane thought that if she worked hard enough, maybe someday she could do that too.

So she tried carving animals out of firewood.

And once, when her parents were giving a party,
she made a very nice mermaid out of butter.

When, at last, she felt she was ready, Jane asked
Pyg if she could be his apprentice. Since she was
already his best friend, naturally he agreed.

So Jane went to work sharpening tools, sweeping
the floor, and helping lug great hunks of stone into
the workshop. In exchange for her help, Pyg taught
her the secrets of his craft.

Now one day Pyg bought a fine block of marble. He studied it for hours, trying to decide what he should carve. It had to be just the right thing, you see, because he had the feeling this was going to be his masterpiece.

Once Pyg got started, he couldn't stop. He worked day and night. Jane had to remind him to eat and sleep. But finally, after weeks of frantic work, Pyg put down his tools.

"Jane," he gasped. "Come look!"

So Jane came. And she looked.

She had to admit it was pretty amazing. Or amazingly pretty. Maybe a little of both. Pyg had carved a beautiful goddess, and she was absolutely perfect. Unfortunately, she was also as cold and heartless as the stone from which she was made.

"It's wonderful," Jane lied.

Pyg stopped working after that. He just sat around all day admiring his goddess. He even gave her presents—a scarf, then a necklace, then a bottle of French perfume. At night he sang to her and told her stories.

"It's only a statue," Jane reminded him.

And of course Pyg knew this. But he couldn't help wishing that his goddess could be more than just a statue. He wished she could be a real, live woman.

One night, while he was telling her a story about a dragon and a princess, Pyg fell asleep. As he lay there dreaming, her hard stone feet seemed to grow soft and warm. They moved a little. She gave him a big shove.

"Move," she said. "I'm coming down."

"Dearest!" cried Pyg, with joy in his heart. "I adore you!"

"Of course you do," said the goddess. "Now get me out of here. I've been a rock for twenty million years and I'm ready for some excitement."

And she was out the door, just like that!

Naturally Pyg followed her. He had no idea where they were going, but he didn't care. He just wanted to look at her. Such pink cheeks she had! Such a perfect little rosebud mouth! Such thick and shiny hair! Pyg sighed with admiration.

"What?" snapped the goddess. "Why are you staring at me?"

"I can't help it," Pyg said. "You're so beautiful!"

"Really?" Now she was interested. "I want to see! Get me a mirror!"

Since Pyg didn't have a mirror handy, he took her to a nearby pond so she could look at her reflection in the water.

"Wow!" she squealed. "You're right! I'm absolutely gorgeous!" Then she fell into the pond with an impressive splash.

"My hair!" she wailed. "It's ruined!"

"No," said Pyg, "it's just wet."

"A lot you know!" screamed the goddess. "My curls are flat! I'm coated with pond scum! Fix it! Now!"

So Pyg and the goddess went to the nearest village, and he bought her a new dress. Then he took her to the beauty shop, where she got a shampoo and blow-dry, a manicure, and a pedicure.

While Pyg was paying the bill and the goddess was admiring her new hairdo in the window, a thought suddenly flew into her head. It had to do with that story Pyg had told her, back when she was still a rock—the one about the princess and the dragon. She decided she looked exactly like the heroine in that story.

"Hey!" she said. "I need you to find me a dragon, pronto! The big kind, with seven heads and huge fangs. Then I want you to fight it for me."

Pyg sighed. The only dragon he knew about was in the middle of a fountain in the market square. It had only one head, but it was big and it was scary. He knew this because he had carved it himself.

"This way," he said.

Back at the studio, Jane arrived to find the door wide open. Then she spotted the empty pedestal. She was so stunned she had to sit down and clear her head.

Was this a good thing or a bad thing, Jane wondered. It was what Pyg had wished for. And she wanted Pyg to be happy. Maybe she had misjudged the goddess. After all, appearances can be deceiving. Why, she might be charming! Friendly! A teller of jokes!

Somehow Jane didn't think so.

"Poor Pyg," she said as she gathered up her carving tools and headed home.

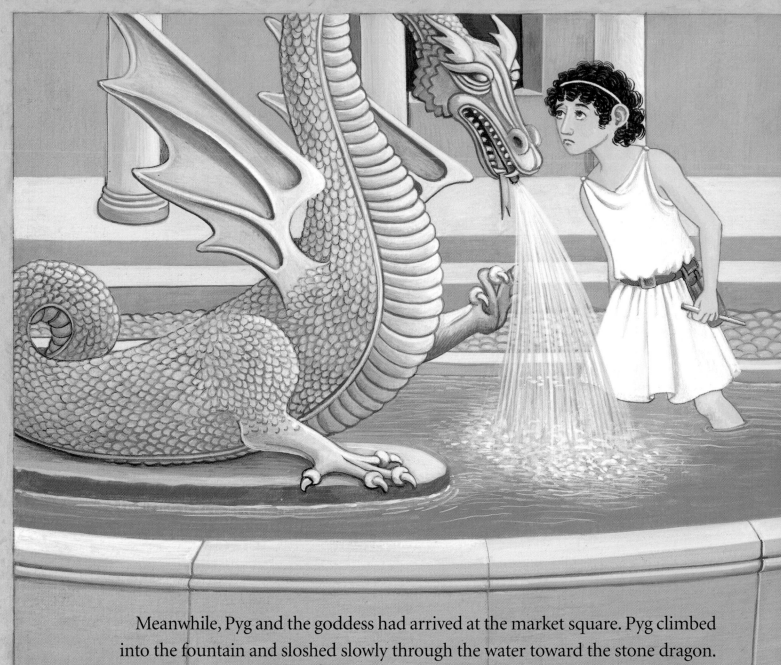

Meanwhile, Pyg and the goddess had arrived at the market square. Pyg climbed into the fountain and sloshed slowly through the water toward the stone dragon. "What's the holdup?" barked the goddess. "Let's get this show on the road!"

So Pyg, trying his best to look like a storybook hero, pulled a chisel out of his leather pouch and made menacing advances upon the stone beast.

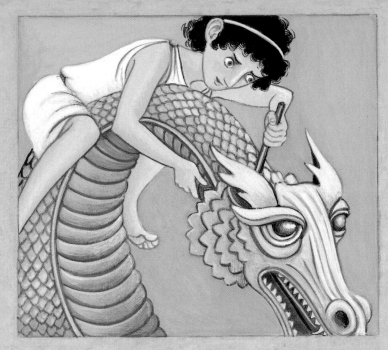

"Take that!" he cried, shimmying up its neck and pretending to stab it.

"Die, you horrible beast!" he screamed, slamming his chisel into the water pipe.

"Is it dead?" asked the goddess.

"Turned to stone," said Pyg, climbing out of the fountain. "Now let's go home."

"To your place? Get real!"

"What's wrong with my place?" asked Pyg. "It's cozy."

"No, it's a dump. I want to live in a house that is big, with lots of gold stuff around. Fancy windows, furniture with curvy legs, velvet curtains. In fact," she said, pointing at the palace that crowned the highest hill, "someplace just like that!"

"It's already occupied," explained Pyg. "The prince lives there."

"Perfect," said the goddess.

Armed guards blocked the entrance to the palace, but the goddess wasn't worried. All she had to do was tilt her head, smile sweetly, and bat her eyelashes at them. They let her right in.

"What about me?" asked Pyg.

"You're all wet," she said, shrugging her shoulders, "and I can handle the rest myself."

Pyg knew she was right on both counts. He didn't even say good-bye.

His heart felt surprisingly light for a guy who had just lost the girl of his dreams.

Now while Pyg was on his way home, Jane was busy working on a sculpture of her own. She thought if Pyg could imagine an ideal companion and bring her to life through art, then so could she.

Only hers didn't have to be perfect. Just loyal and loving, merry and brave.

She was tickled pink with the results.

When she was done, she built a blazing fire, set up the Scrabble board, and put some cider on to warm. Then she got cozy in her favorite chair.

Her new friend came over and laid his head in her lap. She scratched him behind the ears.

And they sat there, contentedly, waiting for Pyg to come home.

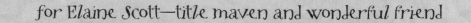

for Elaine Scott—title maven and wonderful friend

This story is based on a famous Greek myth, Pygmalion, in which a sculptor carves a statue of a woman so beautiful that he falls madly in love with her. Aphrodite, the goddess of love, brings the statue to life so Pygmalion can marry her. They live happily ever after.

In 1916 a famous writer, George Bernard Shaw, borrowed this myth and turned it into a play, *Pygmalion*. It was later made into a musical, *My Fair Lady*. In Shaw's version, an arrogant Englishman makes a bet that he can take a poor, ignorant girl off the streets and pass her off as a great lady simply by teaching her to speak like one. He succeeds, and naturally—this being a Pygmalion story—falls in love with his own creation. As to whether they were happy together, Shaw does not say.

In writing my own Pygmalion story, I decided to have a bit of fun with the notions of perfect beauty and misguided love. And after all—aren't there many different kinds of happy endings?

The Trouble with Wishes • Copyright © 2007 by Diane Stanley • Manufactured in China. • All rights reserved. No part of this book may be used or reproduced in any manner whatsoever without written permission except in the case of brief quotations embodied in critical articles and reviews. For information address HarperCollins Children's Books, a division of HarperCollins Publishers, 1350 Avenue of the Americas, New York, NY 10019. • www.harpercollinschildrens.com • Library of Congress Cataloging-in-Publication Data is available. • ISBN-10: 0-06-055451-7 — ISBN-13: 978-0-06-055451-4 • ISBN-10: 0-06-055452-5 (lib. bdg.) — ISBN-13: 978-0-06-055452-1 (lib. bdg.) • Design by Stephanie Bart-Horvath • 1 2 3 4 5 6 7 8 9 10 • ❖ • First Edition